SOMETHING
FOR
CHRISTMAS

by
Palmer Brown

**THE NEW YORK REVIEW
CHILDREN'S COLLECTION**
New York

THIS IS A NEW YORK REVIEW BOOK
PUBLISHED BY THE NEW YORK
REVIEW OF BOOKS
435 Hudson Street, New York, NY 10014
www.nyrb.com

Published by arrangement with HarperCollins Children's
Books, a division of HarperCollins Publishers.

Library of Congress Cataloging-in-Publication Data
Brown, Palmer.
Something for Christmas / by Palmer Brown ; illustrations
by Palmer Brown.
p. cm. — (New York Review Books children's
collection)
Summary: A little mouse searches for just the right
Christmas gift for his mother.
ISBN 978-1-59017-462-3 (alk. paper)
[1. Mice—Fiction. 2. Gifts—Fiction. 3. Christmas—
Fiction. 4. Mother and child—Fiction.] I. Title.
PZ7.B816647So 2011
[E]—dc23
2011012575

ISBN 978-1-59017-462-3

Cover design by Louise Fili Ltd.

Printed in the United States of America on acid-free paper
1 3 5 7 9 10 8 6 4 2

SOMETHING FOR CHRISTMAS

"What are you doing, dear?"
  "It is a secret."

5

"Secrets are better if you share them
a little. So tell Mother why you look
so sad on Christmas Eve."

"I am wondering what to give–
someone–for Christmas."

6

"Well, what would you like to give
this person for Christmas?"

"I could make her a pincushion."

7

"Pincushions are nice. But do you
know how to make a pincushion?"
    "Yes. First you take a piece of
velvet–"

8

"Wait. Do you have a piece of
velvet?"

"No."

9

"Then you cannot make her a
pincushion, can you?"
"No."

"What else could you give this person
for Christmas?"
"I could make her a penwiper."

"Penwipers are nice. But do you
know how to make a penwiper?"
"Yes. First you take a piece of
flannel–"

"Wait. Do you have a piece of
flannel?"

"No."

"Then you cannot make her a
penwiper, can you?"
"No."

14

"What else could you give this person
for Christmas?"

"I could make her a plum pudding."

15

"Plum puddings are nice. But do
you know how to make a plum
pudding?"

"Yes. First you take a dozen
raisins–"

"Wait. Do you have a dozen
raisins?"
"No."

"Then you cannot make her a plum
pudding, can you?"

"No. So I am afraid I have nothing
at all that I can give for Christmas."

"Dear, I know something you have
that only you can give."
"Something of my own?"

"Your very own. Think hard."

"I know! My red carpet-slippers?"

"No. Not your red carpet-slippers.
Think again."

"I know! My blue night-shirt?"

"No. Not your blue night-shirt.
Think again."

"I know! My little jar of whisker-
wax?"

"No. Not your little jar of whisker-wax. Think again."
"I cannot think any more."

"Well, come tell me, why do you want to give this person something for Christmas?"

"Because I love her very much."

"Oh? And have you thought of giving her your love?"
"Is just that enough?"

"Why, that is the very best gift of all, for love is what Christmas is really about!

But do you know how to give this
person your love?"

"Yes. Like this, Mother! For the person I love is you."

"Thank you, dear. That is just what I wanted for Christmas!

31

Now let us see what we can find for
a little mouse I love very much too."

PALMER BROWN was born in Chicago and attended Swarthmore and the University of Pennsylvania. He is the author and illustrator of five books for children, including *Beyond the Pawpaw Trees* and its sequel, *The Silver Nutmeg*; *Cheerful*; and *Hickory*—all forthcoming from The New York Review Children's Collection.